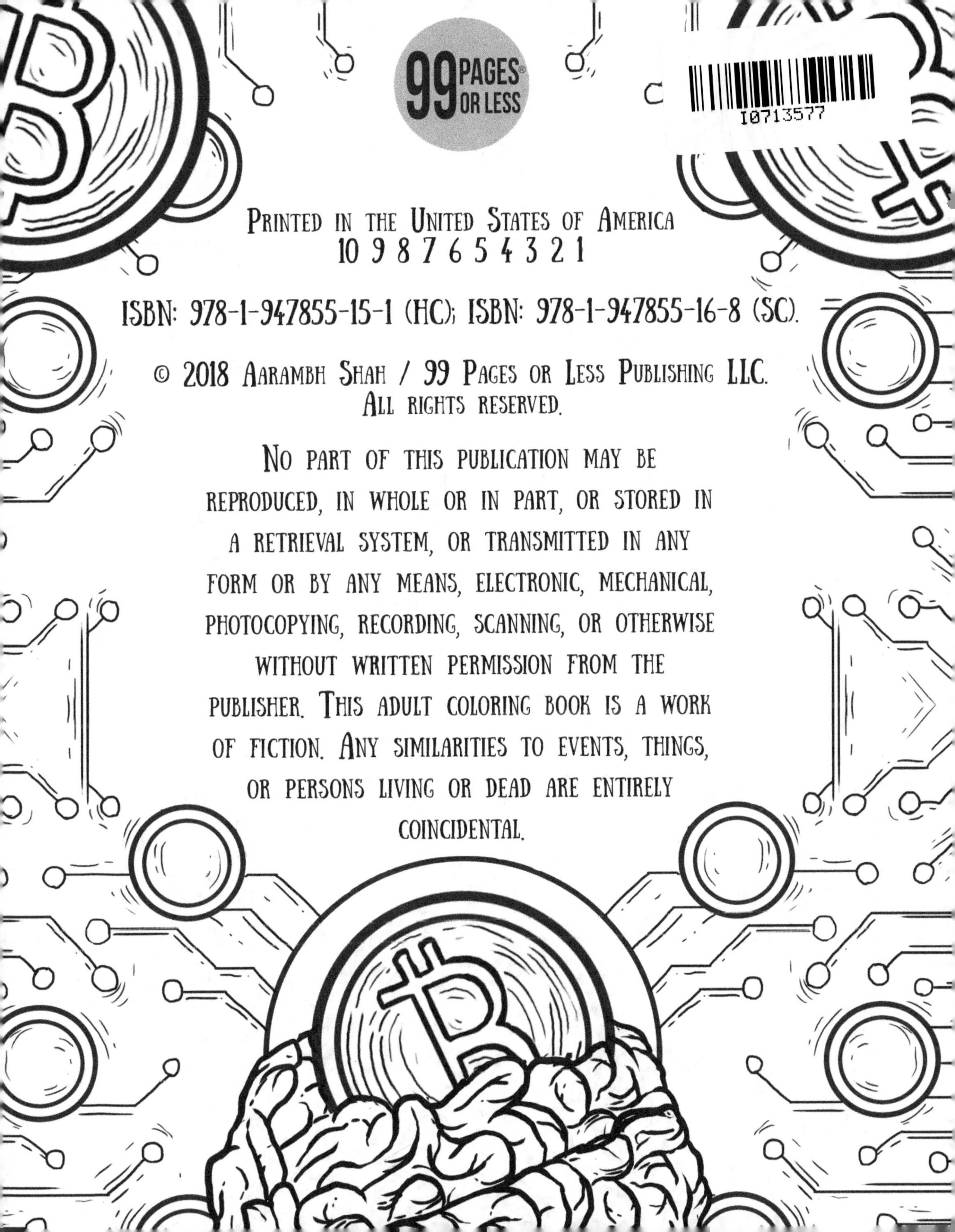

99 PAGES OR LESS

ARE YOU A CRYPTOCURRENCY ZOMBIE?

LEARN THE SLANG !

CRYPTO SLANG BELONGS TO:

____

BLOCK 0

1. AIRDROP
2. ALTCOIN
3. ATH
4. BAGHOLDER
5. BEARWHALE
6. BITCOIN
7. BLOCKCHAIN
8. BLOCKREWARD
9. BTFD

BLOCK 1

10. COLD STORAGE
11. CRYPTOCURRENCY
12. DYOR
13. ELLIOT WAVES
14. FIB RETRACEMENT
15. FLIPPENING
16. FOMO
17. FORK
18. FUD
19. GENESIS BLOCK
20. HODL

BLOCK 2

21. ICO
22. IMO
23. LITECOIN
24. MASTERNODES
25. MAXIMALIST
26. MINING
27. NOOB
28. OCD
29. PRIVATE KEY
30. PUMP N' DUMP

BLOCK 3

31. REKT
32. ROADMAPS
33. SHILL
34. SHITCOIN
35. SMART CONTRACT
36. TO THE MOON
37. WALL
38. WALLET
39. WEAK HANDS
40. WHALE

AIR DROP

ALTCOIN

ATH

BAG HOLDER

BEARWHALE

BITCOIN

BLOCKCHAIN

BLOCK REWARD

BTFD

COLD STORAGE

CRYPTOCURENCY

DYOR

ELLIOT WAVES

.236
.618
.382
FIB
RETRACEMENTS

FLIPPENING

FOMO

FORK

FUD

GENESIS BLOCK

R.I.P
HODL

ICO

IMO

LITECOIN

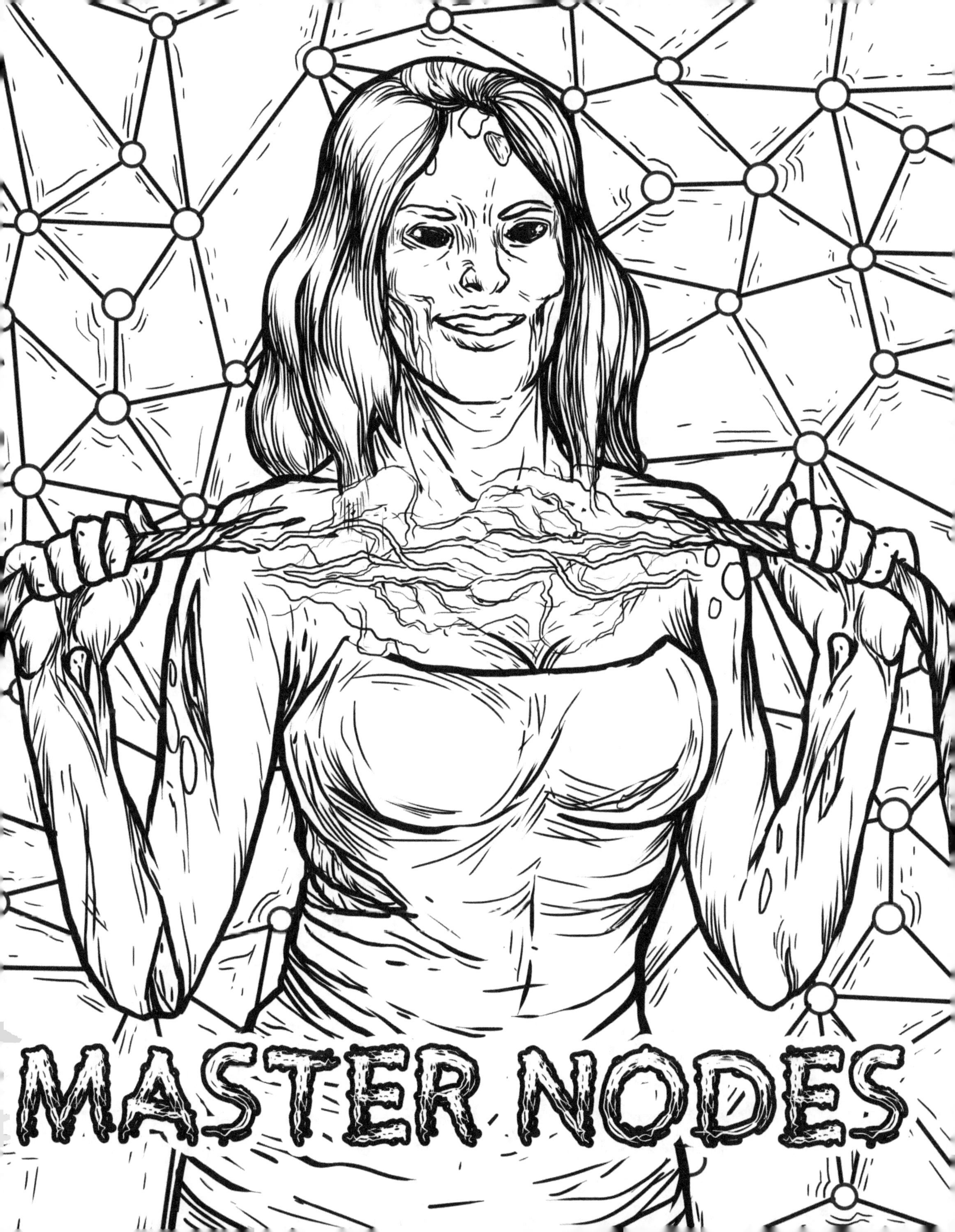
MASTER NODES

MAXIMALIST

MINING

B
NOOB

OCD

PRIVATE KEY

PUMP-N' DUMP

REKT

ROADMAPS

SHILL

SHITCOIN

SMART
CONTRACTS

TO THE MOON

WALL
4669.96
3369.09
5699.96
5269.69
5693.69

WALLET

WEAK HANDS

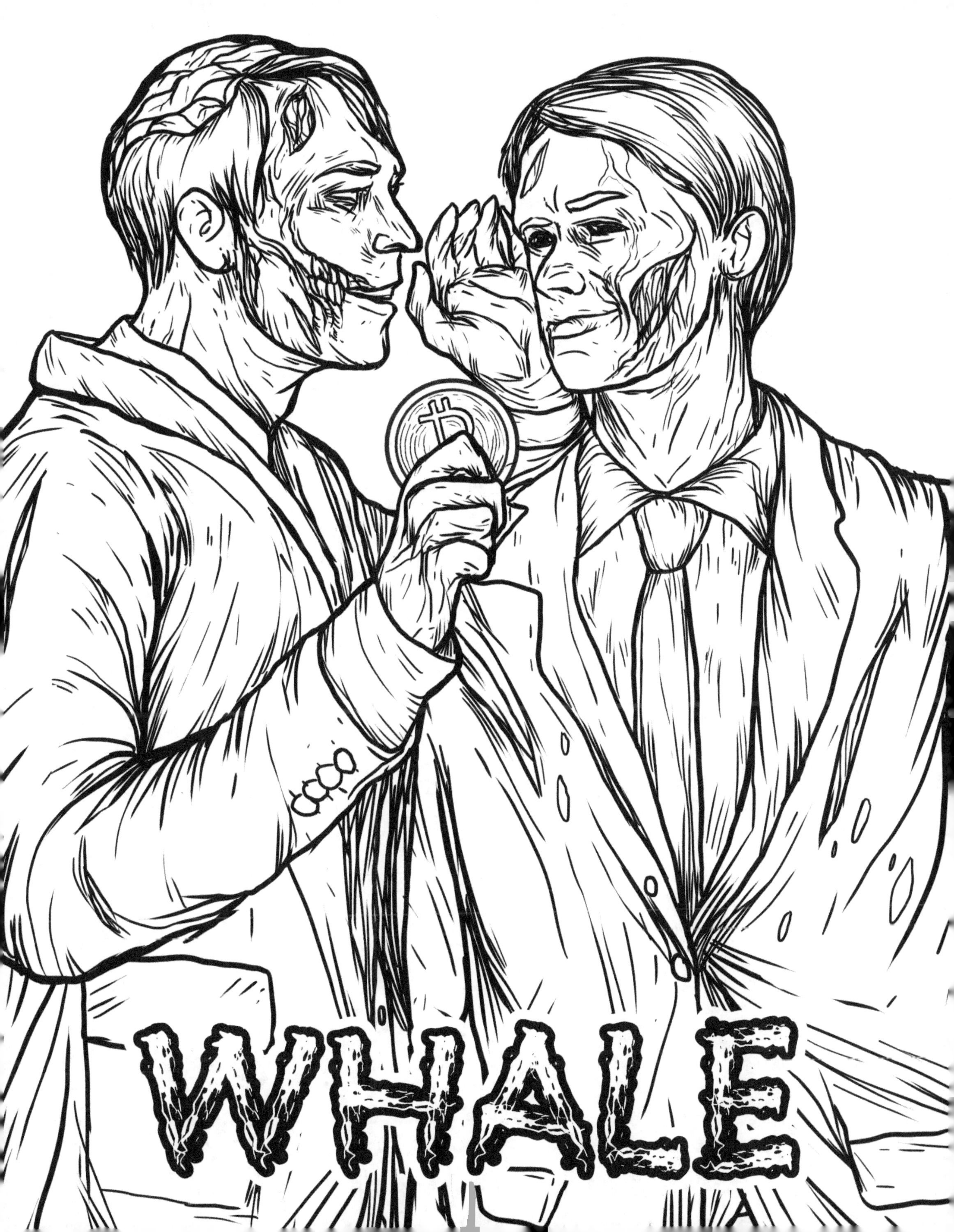

WHALE